P9-DVI-949

WITHDRAWN

The Hungry Giant
of the Tundra

T 162964

VISTA GRANDE
PUBLIC LIBRARY

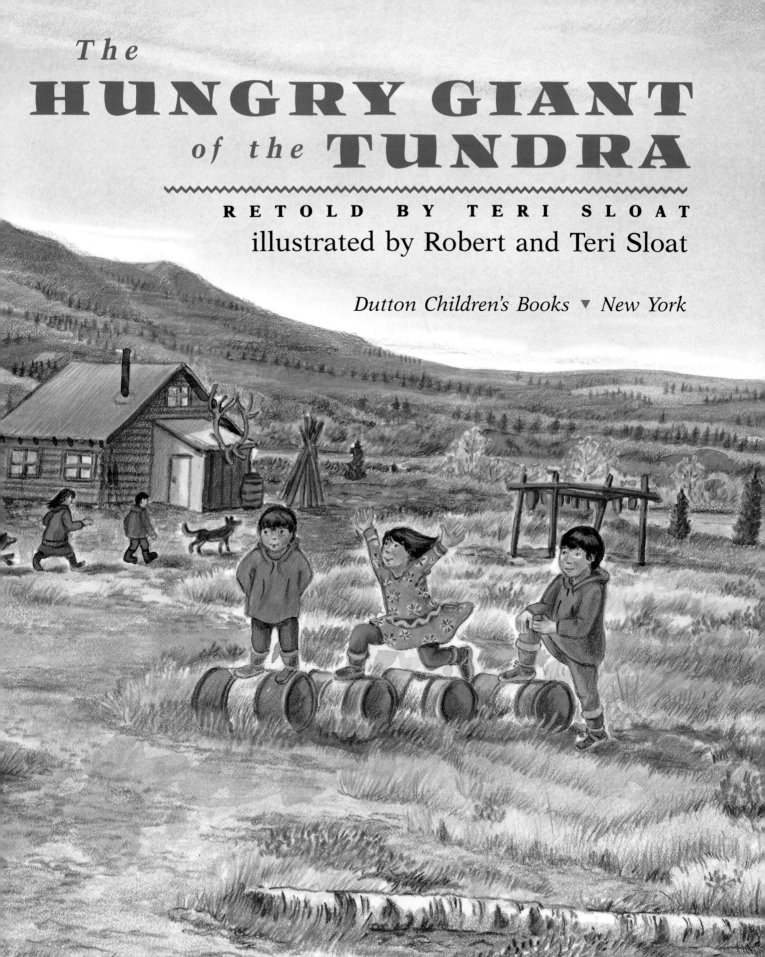

The
HUNGRY GIANT
of the TUNDRA

RETOLD BY TERI SLOAT

illustrated by Robert and Teri Sloat

Dutton Children's Books ▾ *New York*

In memory of Olinka Michael
and with gratitude to Lillian Michael

∿∿∿∿∿∿∿∿∿∿∿∿∿∿∿∿∿∿∿∿∿∿∿∿∿∿∿∿∿∿

RETELLER'S NOTE

In the tradition of Yupik storytelling, tales can serve other purposes in addition to entertainment. Some contain implicit warnings of the consequences of breaking—whether through greediness, laziness, or disobedience—a code of behavior necessary for survival.

Different frightening creatures appear in the tales cautioning children against roaming the tundra. But A·ka·gua·gan·kak, the hungry giant, is a favorite of storytellers. In the telling, his name is said slowly, to imitate someone large and thickheaded plodding across the tundra. We hope the length of the giant's authentic Yupik name is not intimidating to those who want to read the story aloud. The bullets are meant to help separate his name into five pronounceable units: ah·kah·gu-ah·GAHN·kahk. All the *a*'s are pronounced as *ah*'s.

Versions of this story are told throughout Alaska and Canada. This one is from Olinka Michael, a master storyteller in the village of Kwethluk, Alaska. Her daughter, Lillian Michael, wrote it down in Yupik, and it was first published by a federally funded bilingual press and education center in Bethel, Alaska, where both she and I worked. Now, many years later, I am happy to produce a retelling in English for a wider audience.

—Teri Sloat

Text copyright © 1993 by Teri Sloat
Illustrations copyright © 1993 by Robert and Teri Sloat
All rights reserved.

Library of Congress Cataloging-in-Publication Data
Sloat, Teri.
The hungry giant of the tundra/retold by Teri Sloat;
illustrated by Robert and Teri Sloat.—1st ed.
p. cm.
Summary: The hungry giant is tricked out of his delightful supper.
ISBN 0-525-45126-9
1. Eskimos—Legends.   2. Giants—Folklore.   [1. Eskimos—Legends.
2. Giants—Folklore.   3. Indians of North America—Legends.]
I. Sloat, Robert, ill.   II. Title.
E99.E7S524 1993   398.2'089971—dc20   [398.2] [E]   93-12166   CIP   AC

Published in the United States 1993 by Dutton Children's Books,
a division of Penguin Books USA Inc.
375 Hudson Street, New York, New York 10014
Designed by Sara Reynolds
Printed in Hong Kong
First edition
10 9 8 7 6 5 4 3 2 1

In a village far to the north, the children always ran home before A·ka·gua·gan·kak, the hungry giant, came across the tundra, looking for his evening meal. But one night they were having so much fun outside, they pretended not to hear their parents calling them in. Instead, they played farther and farther from the village.

The smallest boy was the first to smell the breath of the giant. In the air he heard the voice of A·ka·gua·gan·kak coming across the hill.

I smell little children warm in the sun.
I'll eat them all, one by one.

The boy ran to the other children. "A·ka·gua·gan·kak is coming," he shouted.

Because he was the smallest, no one paid much attention to him.

But soon, one by one, they too smelled the ugly smell. They heard the giant's voice. They saw the tundra darken with his shadow.

I found little children warm in the sun.
I'll start my dinner with the smallest one.

And right behind the shadow was A·ka·gua·gan·kak!

The children all ran for the village. But the giant reached out and scooped them up, even the smallest one, and carried them off to his favorite eating place.

"Aaahh! What a dinner!" said the giant as he searched his pocket for his knife. But giants are often forgetful. He had left his knife at home.

The hungry giant sat for a long time wondering how to keep his dinner from running away while he went to get his knife.

Then he had an idea. Since giants are not very modest, he took off his trousers and tied the legs together to make a bag. Then, one by one, he dropped all the children, even the smallest one, into the bag.

He tied a knot in his suspenders, hung the trousers in a tall tree, and lumbered off to get his knife.

Now, in the top of that tall tree was a little chickadee singing, *Chick-a-di-di-di, chick-a-di.*

As soon as the giant disappeared over the hill, the children called
to the bird, "Chickadee with your strong beak, fly down and help us!"

Chickadee-with-the-strong-beak flew down and pulled on the knot tied in the suspenders. He pulled and pulled until the knot came untied. Then chickadee held on tight to the suspenders and lowered the children to the ground.

They all scrambled out as fast as they could. But before they ran off, they stuffed the giant's pants full of rocks and grass and sticks.

They held the bag high, and chickadee-with-the-strong-beak tied
the trousers back in the tree.

Then the children ran off as fast as they could through the trees.
Not far away, they came to the bank of a wide river. On the other side
of the river stood a crane dancing on her long legs.

The children shouted, "Crane with your long legs that stretch, help us to the other side!"

Crane-with-the-long-legs fanned out her tail and sat down firmly
on the bank of the wide river. She stretched her long legs until they
reached to the other bank and made a bridge for the children.

One by one, the children walked on crane's legs, until even the
smallest one was across the river.

"Hide in the trees and wait," crane said.

By this time A·ka·gua·gan·kak had returned to the tall tree with his knife. He was **HUNGRY!**

But when he reached into his pants for his dinner, all he pulled out was a rock. He reached in again and pulled out...grass. He reached in *again* and pulled out...a branch. He grabbed his pants and shook them.

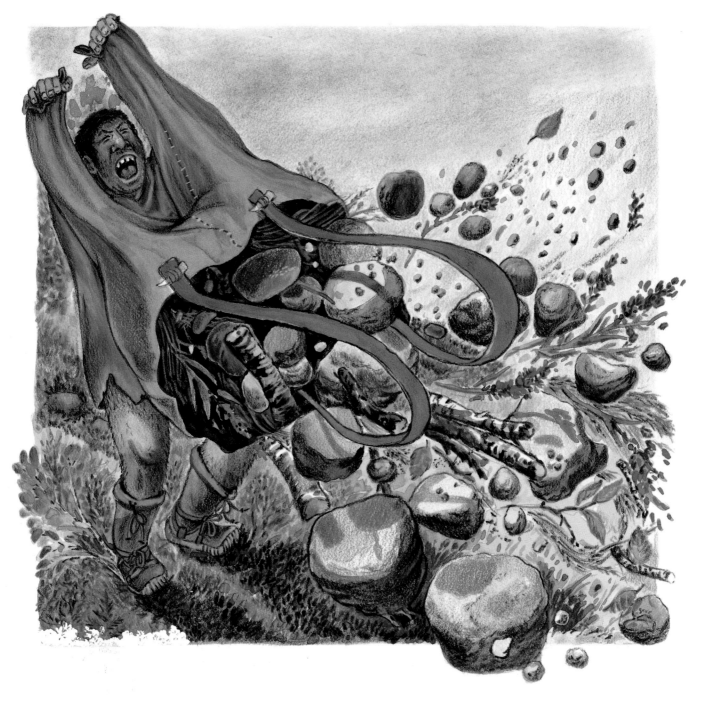

Not even the smallest child was left to eat. The hungry giant was
ANGRY!

He stomped his feet until the tundra shook. Then he took off down
the path after the children.

When he got to the river, he saw crane on the other side, fanning her wings. "Crane-with-the-long-legs," the giant hollered, "stretch out your legs so I can cross the river."

To the children's surprise, crane did as the giant ordered. She stretched her legs out to make a bridge for the giant.

A·ka·gua·gan·kak started across the river. Crane's legs shook under his weight. "Hold still, crane!" roared the giant. Crane steadied her legs, and the hungry giant continued across the water toward the frightened children.

But when he was over the coldest, swiftest, deepest part of the
river, crane pulled her long legs back. With a huge splash,

A·ka·gua·gan·kak fell into the river! And since giants cannot swim, he was carried down the river and to the bottom of the sea.

Crane flew the children back to the village, where their parents were still calling for them. All the children, even the smallest one, ran right home.